The Little Reindeer

Written by Caroline Repchuk * Illustrated by Stephanie Boey

SCHOLASTIC INC.
New York Toronto London Auckland
Sydney Mexico City New Delhi Hong Kong

Little Reindeer gazed in wonder as fat snowflakes floated down and settled softly all around him. It was his first winter and, instead of the sweet grass of summer, the ground was covered in a snowy blanket.

"Come on, Little Reindeer," called his father. "You have much to learn now that winter is here. Today, I will teach you how to find food when there is no more grass to eat."

"That's my daddy," Little Reindeer said proudly to Raccoon, who was watching nearby. "Today, he is teaching me to find food."

"There's a lot more than that to learn if you are going to grow up to be a big, strong reindeer like your father," teased Raccoon. "Why, you haven't even got any antlers yet!"

And it was true. Little Reindeer only had two tiny bumps on the top of his head where his antlers should be. He hurried through the snow after his father.

"Why don't I have antlers like you, Daddy?" he asked, anxiously. "Be patient. Your antlers will grow when they're ready," soothed his father. "Maybe even by the time I get back."

"Get back?" cried Little Reindeer, now more anxious than ever. "Why, where are you going?"

"It's a secret," said his father. "Sometimes grown-up reindeers have special jobs to do, but don't worry – I won't be away for long and your mother will look after you until I get back." And although Little Reindeer pestered him with questions, his father would say no more.

The next morning, Little Reindeer woke to find his father
had already left. He asked his mother over and over where he
had gone, but she just smiled and told him he would find out
all about it when he was older.

But Little Reindeer wanted to know what the secret was NOW!
So, although he had been told many times to stay close to his
mother and the rest of the herd, he decided to set off into the
forest to find his daddy.

Little Reindeer hadn't gone far when he sensed someone watching him from behind a mound of snow. "Is there anyone there?" he called, his voice trembling. But it was only Fox playing in a snowdrift.

"What are you doing out in the forest all alone, Little Reindeer?" asked Fox kindly. "Shouldn't you be with your daddy, learning the ways of reindeer?"

"My daddy has gone away to do a special job," explained Little Reindeer, "and I am going to find him."

"Well, that's very brave of you," said Fox, "but you should find your way home before it gets dark."

Little Reindeer carried on walking through the forest until he saw a great, dark shadow moving amongst the trees. "Perhaps it's my daddy," he thought joyfully.

But the mighty creature wasn't his father – it was Moose who was out in the forest teaching his son to look after his antlers by rubbing them against the bark of the trees.

"My antlers haven't grown yet, but I'm sure my daddy will teach me how to look after them when they do," explained Little Reindeer. "I'm sure he will – and many other things besides," added Moose before he disappeared off through the trees with his son.

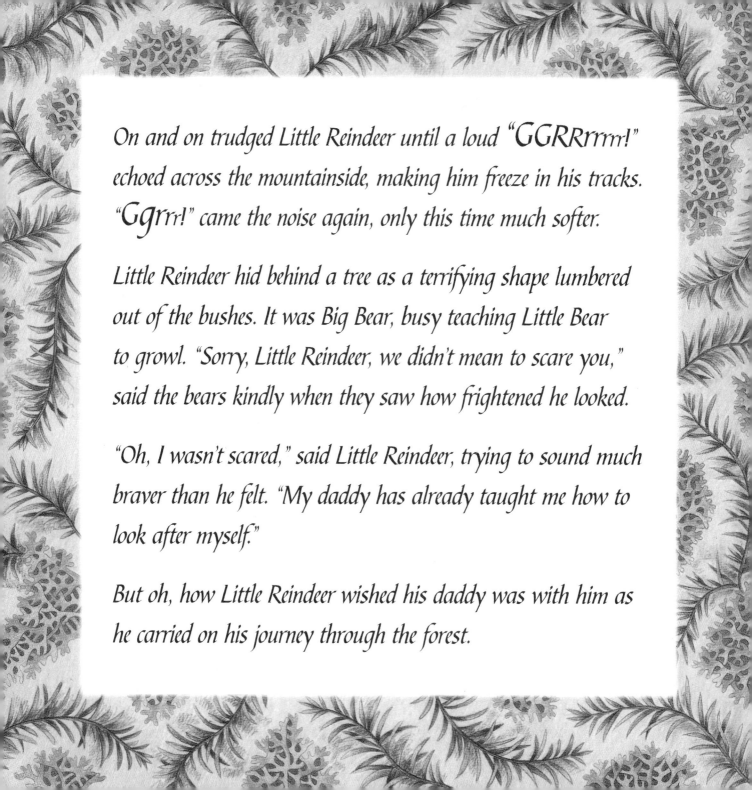

On and on trudged Little Reindeer until a loud "GGRRrrrr!" echoed across the mountainside, making him freeze in his tracks. "Ggrrr!" came the noise again, only this time much softer.

Little Reindeer hid behind a tree as a terrifying shape lumbered out of the bushes. It was Big Bear, busy teaching Little Bear to growl. "Sorry, Little Reindeer, we didn't mean to scare you," said the bears kindly when they saw how frightened he looked.

"Oh, I wasn't scared," said Little Reindeer, trying to sound much braver than he felt. "My daddy has already taught me how to look after myself."

But oh, how Little Reindeer wished his daddy was with him as he carried on his journey through the forest.

As daylight faded, Little Reindeer headed for the shelter of a cave. Inside, Lynx was playing rough-and-tumble with his cub as they settled down for the night. "My daddy always plays with me at bedtime too," said Little Reindeer sadly. "But now he's gone away to do a secret job and I have been trying to find him all day."

"You should go home, Little Reindeer," said Lynx gently. "It will soon be dark and your mother will be worried."

"I'm not going home until I've found my daddy," said Little Reindeer stubbornly, and he went back out into the night to continue his search.

Night had fallen over the mountainside and, although there was a bright moon overhead, Little Reindeer decided he could search no further. Tired and lonely, he curled up beneath a tree to wait for morning.

How he wished he was home with his mummy, and how miserable he was that he had not found his father.

Just then, he heard a noise overhead, a strange tinkling noise, a noise that filled his heart with wonder and hope. And when he looked up, there silhouetted against the moon was a sight that filled him with joy.

At last he knew where his father had been…

It took a long while for Little Reindeer to make his way back home. By the time he got there, the sun was rising over the horizon and his father was already waiting for him. "Where have you been, Little Reindeer?" cried his daddy. "Your mother and I have been so worried."

"Why, I went to look for you," said Little Reindeer happily. "And I saw you. Yes, I really did."

"So now you know what my special job is," said his father smiling. "And one day it will be your special job, too — just as soon as you are old enough and your antlers have grown."

"But they're growing already!" cried Little Reindeer, nuzzling his head against the warm fur of his father's neck. And, sure enough, they were.

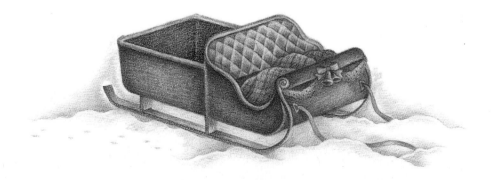

Today, of course, Little Reindeer is no longer little. He grew up to be just as big and strong as his daddy, with a fine pair of antlers, too.

And now, on one very special night every year, he himself sets off to do that very important job. I'm sure you can guess what it is, can't you?

For Max, Archie and their dad, Tim – CR
For Hun Sung, who loves snow – SB

First published in the UK in 2005 by Templar Publishing.

ISBN 978-0-545-33012-1

12 11 10 9 8 7 6 5 4 3 2 1   10 11 12 13 14 15/0

Printed in the U.S.A.   08

First Scholastic printing, December 2010

Designed by Caroline Reeves
Edited by Sue Harris